THE BUG THE DOG

For Epomis beetles everywhere—J. F.

SIMON SPOTLIGHT
An imprint of Simon & Schuster Children's Publishing Division
1230 Avenue of the Americas, New York, New York 10020
This Simon Spotlight edition December 2020
Text and illustrations copyright © 2020 by Jonathan Fenske
SIMON SPOTLIGHT, READY-TO-READ, and colophon are registered
trademarks of Simon & Schuster, Inc.
For information about special discounts for bulk purchases, please contact
Simon & Schuster Special Sales at 1-866-506-1949
or business@simonandschuster.com.
Manufactured in the United States of America 1022 LAK
4 6 8 10 9 7 5
Library of Congress Cataloging-in-Publication Data
Names: Fenske, Jonathan, author, illustrator.
Title: The bug in the bog / by Jonathan Fenske.
Description: New York, New York : Simon Spotlight, 2020. | Audience: Grades K–1. |
Summary: A bug singing happily in a bog and the hungry frog that is
watching are covered by a thick fog, with surprising results.
Identifiers: LCCN 2020011697 | ISBN 9781534477230 (paperback) |
ISBN 9781534477247 (hardcover) | ISBN 9781534477254 (ebook)
Subjects: CYAC: Insects—Fiction. | Bog—Fiction. | Fog—Fiction. | Humorous stories.
Classification: LCC PZ7.F34843 Bug 2020 | DDC [E]—dc23
LC record available at https://lccn.loc.gov/2020011697

THE BUG IN THE BOG

BY JONATHAN FENSKE

Ready-to-Read

Simon Spotlight

New York   London   Toronto   Sydney   New Delhi

See the bug in the bog.

See the bug on a log.
See the bug watch
the muddy bog bubble.

POP!

The bug sits.
The bug sings.
The bug thinks
happy things,

never dreaming

there could be some trouble.

See the frog
in the bog.

See the frog watch the log.
See the frog flash
a big, sneaky smile.

A hungry frog tummy
thinks bog bugs are yummy!

See the frog
and bug bob
for a while!

See the fog
in the bog.

See the fog hide the log,
and the frog,
and the bug,
and the bubbles.

Now no one
can see,

but if that bug
were me,

I would leave
that bog log
on the double!

Hear the
CHOMP!

Hear the
CHEW!

Hear the
SLURP!

Hear the
SWALLOW!

Hear the soft, swampy
bog bubbles
pop in the hollow.

POP!

See the fog
leave the bog.

See the mud.

See the log.

See the bug,
full of frog,
on the log in the bog
with the bubbles!

JONATHAN FENSKE

is the author of many children's books, including *Let's Play, Crabby!* and *Wake Up, Crabby!* (both of which are 2020 Junior Library Guild selections), *Plankton Is Pushy* (a 2017 Junior Library Guild selection), and the Lego picture book *I'm Fun, Too!* His early reader *A Pig, A Fox, and A Box* was a 2016 Theodor Seuss Geisel Honor winner. Jonathan lives in Greenville, South Carolina, with his wife and three daughters.

READING ★ WITH ★ THE ★ STARS!

Simon Spotlight Ready-to-Read books showcase your favorite characters—the stars of these s[...]

At every level, you are a readi[...]

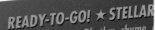

READY-TO-GO! ★ STELLAR[...]
Sight words ★ Word families ★ Rhythm, rhyme,

PRE-LEVEL ONE ★ RISING STAR READE[...]
Shared reading ★ Familiar characters ★ Simple words

LEVEL ONE ★ STAR READER!
Easy sight words and words to sound out ★ Simple plot and dialogue
Familiar topics and themes

LEVEL TWO ★ SUPERSTAR READER!
Longer sentences ★ Simple chapters ★ High-interest vocabulary words

LEVEL THREE ★ MEGASTAR READER!
Longer, more complex story plot and character development
Challenging vocabulary words ★ More difficult sentence structure

See the bug in the bog.
See the frog in the bog.

Find out what happens in this
laugh-out-loud story with an
ending you will not see coming,
from award-winning author and
illustrator Jonathan Fenske!

Find more Ready-to-Read books at
ReadytoRead.com

EBOOK EDITION ALSO AVAILABLE
jonathanfenske.com

A Ready-to-Read Book/Fiction
Simon Spotlight
Simon & Schuster, New York
1220

ISBN 978-1-5344-7723-0 $4.99 U.S./$6.99 Can.

A JUNIOR LIBRARY GUILD SELECTION